DESMOND COLE
GHOST PATROL

SURF'S UP, CREEPY STUFF!

by **Andres Miedoso**

illustrated by **Victor Rivas**

LITTLE SIMON

New York   London   Toronto   Sydney   New Delhi

LITTLE SIMON

An imprint of Simon & Schuster Children's Publishing Division
1230 Avenue of the Americas, New York, New York 10020
First Little Simon hardcover edition May 2018
Also available in a Little Simon paperback edition.
All rights reserved, including the right of reproduction in whole or in part in any form.
LITTLE SIMON is a registered trademark of Simon & Schuster, Inc.,
and associated colophon is a trademark of Simon & Schuster, Inc.
For information about special discounts for bulk purchases, please contact
Simon & Schuster Special Sales at 1-866-506-1949 or business@simonandschuster.com.
The Simon & Schuster Speakers Bureau can bring authors to your live event. For more information
or to book an event contact the Simon & Schuster Speakers Bureau at 1-866-248-3049 or
visit our website at www.simonspeakers.com.
Designed by Steve Scott
Manufactured in the United States of America 0418 FFG
2 4 6 8 10 9 7 5 3 1
Library of Congress Cataloging-in-Publication Data
Names: Miedoso, Andres, author. | Rivas, Victor, illustrator.
Title: Surf's up, creepy stuff! / by Andres Miedoso ; illustrated by Victor Rivas.
Other titles: Surf is up, creepy stuff!
Description: First Little Simon paperback edition. | New York : Little Simon, 2018.
Series: Desmond Cole ghost patrol ; #3 | Summary: "Desmond and Andres battle
beach bullies who also happen to be creepy monsters"—Provided by publisher.
Identifiers: LCCN 2017047478 (print) | LCCN 2017057860 (eBook) | ISBN 9781534418035 (eBook)
ISBN 9781534418011 (paperback) | ISBN 9781534418028 (hardcover)
Subjects: | CYAC: Bullies—Fiction. | Monsters—Fiction. | Beaches—Fiction.
| Haunted places—Fiction. | Ghosts—Fiction. | Friendship—Fiction.
African Americans—Fiction.| Hispanic Americans—Fiction.
BISAC: JUVENILE FICTION / Action & Adventure / General. | JUVENILE FICTION /
Imagination & Play. | JUVENILE FICTION / Readers / Chapter Books.
Classification: LCC PZ7.1.M518 (eBook) | LCC PZ7.1.M518 Sur 2018 (print)
DDC [Fic]—dc23
LC record available at https://lccn.loc.gov/2017047478

CONTENTS

CHAPTER ONE

A DAY AT THE BEACH

When people say something is "a day at the beach," they usually mean it was easy. Not me.

When I think about a day at the beach, I think about the hot sun burning the top of my head until I'm melting like a Popsicle.

I think about the sand burning the bottoms of my bare feet until I'm hopping around like a bunny. And I think about how sand gets everywhere: in my hair, in my shorts, even in my mouth. It's so gross!

I think about the birds and how they always want to eat everything you have. *Everything!* The last time I went to the beach, a bird tried to eat my swimsuit . . . and I was still wearing it! Talk about embarrassing!

A day at the beach also means dealing with the ocean. Ugh. Are there people who like spending a day getting salt water in their eyes? Not to mention how creepy the ocean is, with all that slimy seaweed and

jellyfish and *whatever else* is under there. And don't get me started on the crabs and sharks and squids.

Seriously, who would want to spend the day at the beach?

I'll tell you who: Desmond Cole. Of course, with Desmond, there's no chance a day at the beach will be easy. No chance at all!

CHAPTER TWO

YOU LOSE!

It all started on a sunny weekend morning.

I was playing my favorite video game, *Safety Zone*. If you haven't played it, this is what it's about: You are traveling through a strange world. The goal of the game is to stay away from danger and get to the safety zone . . . well, *safely*.

Of course, it's easy to get lost. Then you have to decide what to do.

Take a path in the dark forest? Nope. There's a *dragon* hiding there.

YOU LOSE!

Take an easy shortcut over the old bridge? Oops. There's an *ogre* waiting on the other side.

That's why I always watch out for danger and never take any risks in the game. I just like to get to the safety zone in one piece.

Playing this game relaxed me.

But that day, the peaceful feeling didn't last long. Before I knew it, danger was knocking on my door.

It was Desmond Cole, my neighbor

and best friend. "My family is going to the beach," he told me. "Do you want to come with us?"

"Um, I was just playing my video game, and—"

"Oh no way, mister," my mom said. "It's so beautiful outside. You're not sitting in the house all day."

And just like that, the day I had planned was over. I had no choice. It was time to leave the *Safety Zone*. Because when my mom said "It's so beautiful outside," what she meant was *No more video games for you.*

I went upstairs and changed. Then my dad sprayed me with SPF 1,000, because you can never be too careful, right?

Desmond's parents were already outside packing the car. It was so crowded with stuff that it didn't look like there was any room left for us.

"Check this out," Desmond said, opening the door to the back seat. All I could see were huge floats everywhere. "It's a secret compartment," he said, and he crawled underneath the beach junk.

I followed him, and sure enough, Desmond had made himself a little cove. It was pretty comfy in there too.

"How far away is the beach?" I asked him. It was my first time going since I moved to Kersville.

"It's not too far," Desmond said. "You're going to love Dreary Beach. It has the softest sand, the warmest water, and the biggest waves!"

Dreary Beach? Didn't "dreary" mean "dull and boring"? What kind of name was that for a beach?

Before I could ask, Zax floated
into the car. He was the ghost that
lived with me, but he wasn't scary.
He was just kind of annoying like a
little brother. "Wow!" he said. "You're
going to Dreary Beach! Do you have
room for a ghost?"

Do you have room for a ghost? A question like that used to scare me, but not anymore. Not when it came to a ghost like Zax.

"I'm sorry, Zax," Desmond said. "Take a look around. There's barely room for Andres and me! Plus, my

parents are cool, but they're not, like, ghosts-in-the-car cool. Maybe next time, okay?"

Zax nodded. "I get it. Have fun surfing. Hang ten, dudes!"

As soon as Zax was gone, I asked Desmond, "So, does that mean we're going to a dull, boring beach with no ghosts?"

"I guess," Desmond said.

Now Dreary Beach sounded like it was going to be perfect. The only problem was that there weren't many dull and boring places in Kersville. I had learned that the hard way.

CHAPTER THREE

DREARY BEACH

"That's weird," Desmond's mom said when we arrived at Dreary Beach.

Weird? That wasn't what I wanted to hear. My heart started pounding. I poked my head out from under the floats and looked out the window.

The parking lot was practically
empty, and when I looked at the
ocean, there weren't a lot of people.

"I don't understand," Mrs. Cole
said. "I thought it would be crowded
on a beautiful day like this."

I swallowed, worried. "How wild?" I asked. I needed to know what to expect. Was there a giant octopus waiting to grab us in its slippery arms? Were there *land sharks*?

Cool! I thought. It was almost like having the beach all to ourselves. What could be better than that?

I couldn't believe how much stuff the Coles had packed. There was a tent, a solar-powered generator, a wagon, a table, a computer, rafts, coolers, chairs, speakers, floats, buckets, shovels, towels, fans, sunscreen, and even a minifridge! Don't ask me how they fit all of it into their car, but they did.

And we had to carry everythi_ down the long wooden walkway th_ went over a set of sand dunes. "The_ don't want anyone walking on these dunes," Desmond said. "They want to protect the wildlife living here."

My eyes opened wide as I looked around.

Desmond laughed. "Calm down, Andres," he said. "I was just talking about wildlife like birds and deer and turtles. There's nothing to worry about."

I let out a sigh of relief. Once again, my mind was running wild. But can you blame me? This is Kersville, after all.

Since the beach was pretty empty, we had no trouble finding the perfect spot. And that was when the Coles got to work setting up everything they brought. Before I knew it, they had built a tent with all the comforts of home.

I looked around the beach. There were a few other families on the sand and surfers riding the waves. *Too bad Zax couldn't come*, I thought. *He would have loved this.*

"What should we do first?" I asked Desmond.

He held up a bucket and shovel. "I challenge you to a haunted sand-castle building contest!"

CHAPTER FOUR

HAUNTED SANDCASTLES

Let me tell you, the Dreary Beach sand is the best sandcastle-building sand in the whole wide world. First of all, it's not hot. It doesn't burn your feet. In fact, it feels nice and cool when you touch it.

Not only that, but the sand on

Dreary Beach really sticks together. Desmond brought tons of buckets, and no matter which he used, the sand always stayed in the shape. Even the crazy shapes worked.

In fact, the sand was so perfect that Desmond and I were building the two biggest sandcastles ever in no time flat. They were so big that we could almost fit inside them.

Other kids on the beach gathered around to watch us work. "What are you guys building?" one girl asked.

Desmond tried to hide a sly smile. "Haunted sandcastles."

"No, you're not," the girl said, and some of the other kids shook their heads. Nobody believed us. But they stayed and watched as we finished.

When I put the flag on my last guard post, the kids actually started applauding.

"Are your castles really haunted?" a boy asked.

"No," I answered. "But if they were, they would be haunted by the, um, *ocean ghost*." It was the only thing I could think of.

"For real?" the boy asked.

"Yeah," I said. "The ocean ghost travels around from one sandcastle to the next, searching for its perfect home."

Desmond smiled and added, "And if you're not careful, it might go home with *you*!"

The boy's eyes widened, but some of the other kids tried to laugh. It was a worried laugh, though. Desmond's face looked so serious that I started to feel a little nervous too. And I was the one who had made up the ocean ghost.

"Don't believe me?" Desmond asked the kids. "If you want to see the ocean ghost, do this: Look at the water and say, 'Ocean ghost, ocean ghost, let me see you. Ocean ghost, ocean ghost, let me free you.'"

Some of the kids laughed again, but one of the girls turned around to face the sea and said,  "Ocean ghost, ocean ghost, let me see you. Ocean ghost, ocean ghost, let me free you."

And that's when it happened! A real ghost popped out of Desmond's sandcastle!

The kids ran screaming down the beach. Even from far away, I still heard one high-pitched scream. Then I realized it was coming from *me*!

Desmond laughed so hard that he fell down. The ghost from the castle was none other than Zax.

He looked at me with the saddest eyes. "I'm sorry, Andres. Desmond thought this would be a very funny prank, and it *was*, right?"

I couldn't answer him right then. My heart was too busy trying to get back to its normal speed. Not that it ever would.

CHAPTER FIVE

SURF'S UP, CREEPY STUFF

"I can't believe you would scare me like that!" I yelled at Zax. "I thought you were my friend! And how did you get here? You couldn't fit in the car."

Zax smirked. "I'm a ghost. I can fit anywhere. Watch this."

He flew over to the teeniest-tiniest

shell and shrank himself right into it. Then he popped back out. "Pretty cool, right?"

I nodded because it was.

"Sorry, Andres," he said again. "Why don't we go surf? Check out those waves!"

"And look how much fun those surfers are having," Desmond said.

They did look like they were having a great time. Then I smiled. I didn't come here to be mad, and it wasn't too late to make this beach day super fun.

We all ran back to Desmond's tent. Well, Zax didn't run. He just kind of floated. While they grabbed a surfboard and a bodyboard, I took a big pineapple-shaped float.

On the way out, I noticed some birds on top of the tent. "What are they doing up there?" I asked Desmond.

"I don't know," he said. "They're probably looking for food. Too bad my mom is cooking. They never eat anything she makes."

Zax gagged a little bit. He tried Mrs. Cole's lasagna once. It was unforgettable . . . in a bad way!

We raced down to the water and splashed our way in. Just like the sand, the water was perfect. And I didn't feel any of the slimy things around my ankles. I was really loving Dreary Beach.

Zax jumped on the surfboard, and he caught a wave right away. I don't know how, but he was an excellent surfer!

Desmond caught the next wave on his bodyboard and rode it all the way in. It looked like so much fun.

I waited for the next perfect wave with my pineapple-shaped float. Riding the waves looked scary, but I wanted to try it.

Then some of the other surfers floated over to me. I waved hello, and they waved back. But as they got closer, I knew something really weird was going on.

Their hands were webbed.

Webbed!

I figured they were wearing a new kind of surfing outfit, but then one of them leaped out of the water. He had green skin, a fishy face, and sharp teeth!

I paddled on my float and swam away. I could hear them hiss behind me. Then a creature reached out and unplugged my float.

The air zizzed out of my pineapple so fast, I went flying into the air. I flew so high and so far that I crashed right into my perfect haunted sand-castle, flattening it out.

Great, I thought, trying to catch my breath. *Now I have sand in my swimsuit* and *monsters in my ocean.*

ay!" I said.

dded. "That's right, but ersurfers hate sharing the hey try to chase everybody

at's not nice," Desmond said. ary Beach is supposed to be for yone. There's no way I'm leaving."

MERSURFER POP UP

Before I could stand up, Desmond and Zax came sailing through the air to join me. They crashed into Desmond's haunted sandcastle.

As Desmond sat there, I asked him, "Did you see those surfers? They're monsters!"

Zax shook his ghost head. "No, they're not monsters. They're mer-surfers."

"Mersurfers?" Desmond and I repeated.

Zax planted his surfboard into the

sand and filled us in on everyth he knew about these creatures. told us that mersurfers lived in th deepest, darkest part of the ocean and that they only came out on perfect beach days.

Zax looked at us, worried. "We have to pack up our stuff and go home right now," he said. "They might come ashore."

Thinking about that made my heart slip into my stomach.

Just then a giant wave crashed, splashing over Desmond and me. When I opened my eyes, there was a mersurfer standing right next to us. He raised his green slimy arms, and the next thing we knew he was chasing us and the other kids down the beach.

CHAPTER SIX

MERSURFER POP UP

Before I could stand up, Desmond and Zax came sailing through the air to join me. They crashed into Desmond's haunted sandcastle.

As Desmond sat there, I asked him, "Did you see those surfers? They're monsters!"

Zax shook his ghost head. "No, they're not monsters. They're mersurfers."

"Mersurfers?" Desmond and I repeated.

Zax planted his surfboard into the

sand and filled us in on everything he knew about these creatures. He told us that mersurfers lived in the deepest, darkest part of the ocean and that they only came out on perfect beach days.

"Like today!" I said.

Zax nodded. "That's right, but listen. Mersurfers hate sharing the beach. They try to chase everybody away."

"That's not nice," Desmond said. "Dreary Beach is supposed to be for everyone. There's no way I'm leaving."

Zax looked at us, worried. "We have to pack up our stuff and go home right now," he said. "They might come ashore."

Thinking about that made my heart slip into my stomach.

Just then a giant wave crashed, splashing over Desmond and me. When I opened my eyes, there was a mersurfer standing right next to us. He raised his green slimy arms, and the next thing we knew he was chasing us and the other kids down the beach.

All the families and people sun-bathing scattered, screaming. But when we passed the Coles' tent, his parents were inside dancing to their beach music. They had no idea what was going on!

We kept running, making it all the way up to the pier. That was when the mersurfer stopped chasing us. He turned around and went back toward his buddies in the water.

On the pier, Desmond and I tried to catch our breath. Even Zax was breathing hard, and he's a ghost!

"That was crazy!" I said, panting like a dog.

"I know," Desmond agreed. "Scaring people at the beach isn't right."

I raised one eyebrow. "Really? You guys scared *me* at the beach."

"That's different," Desmond said. "We're your friends. These monsters are up to no good. And we are not going to let them take Dreary Beach away from us."

We. I knew Desmond was talking about the Ghost Patrol.

It was official. The battle for the beach was on!

CHAPTER SEVEN

THE HOT DOG BIRD

"First things first," Desmond said. "We need to eat."

I followed him over to a hot dog stand. How could he be thinking about food at a time like this? We were just chased off the beach by a mersurfer of all things!

Then he handed me a hot dog, and my stomach did a happy dance. I guess fear makes me hungry!

We ate our hot dogs as we walked down the pier. Desmond Cole always had a plan, and this time, I started to

figure out what he was thinking. The pier stretched over the water, and from there, we could see the whole beach and the ocean . . . including the mersurfers.

Most of the creatures were in the waves, shredding on their surfboards. A few other mersurfers were scaring people away. It was something crazy to see. Whenever the people ran away, they totally ended up scaring the birds.

The weird thing was that the mersurfers were only bothering people at one part of the beach. Other people in other places were left alone to swim and have fun.

"That area must be the best surfing spot," Zax said.

We kept walking toward the end of the pier where people were fishing. Some birds sat on the handrails, squawking. It almost sounded like they were talking to one another.

I was about to take a bite of my hot dog when one of those birds swooped down and stole it right out of my hands! "Hey!" I screamed. "That's mine!"

I tried to swat it away, but another bird swooped down and grabbed my hair. "Aaaargh!" I screamed.

Sand in my shorts, monsters on the beach. And now birds in my hair. I'd had enough of this beach day.

Suddenly the strangest thing happened. All the birds flew away. Then every single fishing pole yanked forward, like each one had caught a fish at the same time.

But the fishers weren't excited. They looked over into the water, screamed, and ran away.

What now? I thought.

A second later, I saw it. Mersurfers were climbing up the fishing lines and onto the pier. Everyone ran—fast!

A bird landed on the handrail. Yes, it was the same one that had stolen my hot dog and held it in its little beak. The mersurfers surrounded that bird and tried to scare it, but it wasn't going anywhere. It was too busy eating.

When it was done, the hot dog

bird flapped its wings, and all the mersurfers freaked out. Like surfers jumping from a bad wave, those sea monsters totally bailed!

I looked at Desmond. He had his thinking face on. I could tell that he was putting some mersurfer-size puzzle pieces together.

CHAPTER EIGHT

TOTES NOT CHILL

A few minutes later, Desmond and I were back in his parents' mega-tent. Desmond searched through a set of drawers. "Those mersurfers are up to something," he said, pulling out big colorful beach towels. "I don't think it's just about surfing the waves."

"What do you mean?" I asked.

"I mean, why would they scare people away from the pier if all they wanted was a place to surf?" he asked.

"Maybe they just want to be left alone," I suggested.

Desmond shook his head. "Then why haven't they scared everyone from the rest of the beach? Why didn't they scare my parents?"

I didn't have an answer, but how was I supposed to understand a bunch of mersurfers?

Desmond closed the drawer. "I think they're trying to keep us from something. This tent is too far away from whatever it is, so they're leaving us alone."

"Maybe we should stay here then, where it's safe," I said.

But I knew what Desmond was going to say before he even said it. "The Ghost Patrol needs to figure out what those mersurfers are up to." Then he threw a beach towel in my direction. "Follow me."

The plan was simple.
And a little nuts! Zax
shrank down, tucked
himself into a shell,
and hopped along the
sand. He was our lookout.
    As for Desmond and me,
we were lying on the sand with our
beach towels spread out on top of us.

It was all about camouflage. Most of the mersurfers were in the water, so Desmond and I just looked like beach towels. And there were a lot of other towels left behind on the sand, thanks to those creatures.

A small group of mersurfers gathered on the beach. When they weren't looking, Zax would let us know it was safe to sneak closer to them. If one of the mersurfers was going to turn around, Zax would signal us again, and back under the towels we'd go.

Ugh! It will take days or even weeks *to get all the sand off me!* I thought.

Once we were finally close enough to the mersurfers, we could hear them talking.

"This evening, when the sun is low," one of them said. "That's when we strike."

I held my breath. *They're making a plan—but a plan for what?*

As I inched a little closer to hear them, a huge gust of wind howled. The breeze kicked up my towel and blew it away.

If you don't like having sand in your shorts, then you will definitely not like having sand in your shorts while looking up at a bunch of mer-surfers. It was a nightmare!

Then one of them spoke to me, but it didn't hiss or growl. It sounded kind of . . . cool. "Yo, little dude. It's, like, totes not chill to sneak up on other dudes, dude!"

I stared at the mersurfer. I didn't know what to say because it was right.

The others bared their teeth at me. They were trying to scare me, but it wasn't going to work this time.

I remembered that hot dog bird on the pier. It made those mersurfers run away just by being a bird.

I didn't have any wings to flap, so I did the next best thing.

CAAAAWWWW!

It was my best crow noise, and let me tell you, it worked. If you ever find yourself surrounded by a group

of mersurfers, all you have to do is flap your arms and caw like a crow.

Those monsters bolted faster than lightning!

Desmond saw the whole thing. "Hmm," he said. "It looks like we're going to need a new plan."

CHAPTER NINE

THE DUNE OCTOPUS

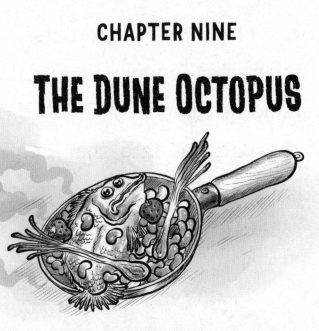

Back at the Coles' beach tent, something smelled . . . fishy. It wasn't the mersurfers this time. Desmond's mom was cooking.

We held our noses tight and ran upstairs. (Yes, the tent actually had an upstairs!) We peeked out the plastic window with binoculars. The mersurfers had come back, and they were making a bonfire.

"If we can get into that bonfire party, then we can stop their evil plan," said Desmond.

I gulped a loud gulp. "Maybe we should just let them enjoy their evil plan and go home?"

Nothing was going to get me out there again. Well, almost nothing.

"Boys! Dinner is ready!" It was Mrs. Cole calling from downstairs.

This time my stomach gurgled a loud gurgle. "Like I was saying, let's catch some mersurfers . . . and maybe skip dinner."

Desmond nodded and yelled, "Thanks, Mom. Can we get our food to go? We want to eat on the beach."

Then he turned to me and asked, "Have you ever been scuba diving?

Desmond and I held our bags of food as we walked across the sand in wetsuits. The suits really made us look like the mersurfers.

Zax flew next to us. "Are you sure this is going to work?"

"No," Desmond said. "But I'm running out of ideas."

We got to the bonfire and tried to blend in. And guess what? It worked! Nobody noticed two kids and a

ghost. Instead, most of the mersurfers were focused on clearing a path
in the sand.

That was when I felt a tap on my shoulder. "Okay, dudes, like, follow me," the mersurfer said. "The little ones are going to make a break for it soon. We need to make sure the dunes are bird-free. You dig?"

I didn't dig. I had no idea what he was talking about! But still, I said, "Totally, um, dude."

The creature smiled. "Radical, little human dude."

Our secret was out! Oh, who were
we fooling? We didn't look anything
like mersurfers in these wetsuits.
Zax, Desmond, and I were busted!

Then the mersurfer put its arms around Desmond and me. "Relax. It's cool, little human dudes and ghost bud. We could use your help."

It took us to the dunes where the wildlife lived. Then it pointed toward some tall grass and the sand started moving like something was under it.

I totally freaked out. Because I knew exactly what was hiding in the ground: *a giant dune octopus!*

CHAPTER TEN

A RAD DAY AT THE BEACH

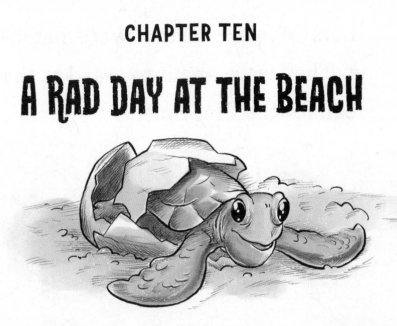

Desmond grabbed hold of me. "Chill out and look."

Slowly, a bunch of tiny crawly things climbed out of the sand. And they weren't dune octopus tentacles. They were baby turtles!

I couldn't believe my eyes.

Lots of baby turtles were hatching. They were about to crawl to the ocean for the first time.

"Listen, little human dudes," the mersurfer said. "I know you two are the same ones who built those great sandcastles earlier. Sorry we had to wreck them, but they were in the turtles' path."

Now it all made sense! The mersurfers were guarding the baby sea
turtles. They wanted to make sure
the babies made it to the water
safely.

"We aren't evil, I promise," the
mersurfer continued. "We don't
have anything against people. But
birds are another story." It shivered.

Desmond snapped his fingers. "Aha! Mersurfers are scared of birds. So when you scared us and we ran away, we scared the birds."

"Exactly!" said the mersurfer as he relaxed. "We need to make sure these little turtle dudes make it to the ocean safe and sound."

Desmond smiled. "Don't worry. Andres and I can help."

And we did. As the baby sea turtles made their way from the dunes, Desmond and I started throwing little pieces of his mom's food at the curious birds. As soon as they smelled it, those birds turned green and flew off. Pretty soon, they all stayed far away from the food *and* the turtles.

Desmond, Zax, and I watched as the baby turtles waded into their new ocean home. Then we cheered. It was the best *beach day* ever!

Turns out, Dreary Beach is not so dreary after all. Actually, there's no better beach.

Desmond, Zax, and I go back whenever we can. We are getting a lot better at surfing, though I'm sure that's because the mersurfers are great teachers.

The only gross thing is that the mersurfers actually love Desmond's mom's cooking. Sushi macaroni, tuna-fish ice cream, olive–peanut butter surprise—you name it, they love it. It makes no sense at all, but I'm glad his mom's food makes them happy.

As for me, I guess you can say I changed too. Now I know that a day at Dreary Beach can be . . . as the mersurfers say, rad!